KT-474-556

This book belongs to:

....

....

Quarto Knows

Quarto is the authority on a wide range of topics.

Quarto educates, entertains and enriches the lives of our readers—enthusiasts and lovers of hands-on living.

www.quartoknows.com

Author and Illustrator: Steve Smallman
Editor: Harriet Stone
Designer: Victoria Kimonidou

© 2018 Quarto Publishing plc

First published in 2018 by QED Publishing,
an imprint of The Quarto Group.
The Old Brewery, 6 Blundell Street,
London N7 9BH, United Kingdom.
T (0)20 7700 6700 F (0)20 7700 8066
www.QuartoKnows.com

All rights reserved. No part of this publication may be reproduced, stored in a retrieval system, or transmitted in any form or by any means, electronic, mechanical, photocopying, recording, or otherwise, without the prior permission of the publisher, nor be otherwise circulated in any form of binding or cover other than that in which it is published and without a similar condition being imposed on the subsequent purchaser.

A catalogue record for this book is available from the British Library.

ISBN 978 1 78493 481 1

9 8 7 6 5 4 3 2

Manufactured in Shenzhen, China

HH102018

FSC
www.fsc.org

MIX
Paper from
responsible sources
FSC® C017606

ASTROMOUSE

by STEVE SMALLMAN

QED

"Look, Mum!" cried Pip excitedly.
"I can see a mouse! There's a
mouse on the moon!"

"Where?" asked Mum.

"There, look!"
insisted Pip.

"Oh, yes," said Mum
(although she couldn't
see anything at all).

"Well, I'm not surprised," she added.
"People do say that the moon is made of cheese."

"Stinky cheese?!" gasped Pip.

Stinky cheese was his
favourite meal - ideally
with biscuit crumbs on top!

"Well, maybe," chuckled Mum.

"Can I live on the moon?"
Pip asked.

"I don't think so Pip -
it's too far away.
Time to go to sleep
now. I'll see you
in the morning."

But Pip was too excited to sleep.
He crept outside. The moon
was shining big and bright just
above the top of Windy Hill.

"I wonder if it really
is made of stinky
cheese," thought Pip.

"If I can just make it to
the top of the hill and
break off a little piece..."

Once at the top, Pip jumped up and down as high as he could, but he still couldn't reach the moon.

"Can I live on the moon today, Mum?"
Pip asked at breakfast the next day.

"You would need to be an
astronaut with a space rocket
to fly to the moon," said Mum.

"What's an as... tro... nut?" asked Pip.

Mum showed him a book with pictures
of rocket ships and astronauts in it.

"Look Mum,

I'M AN ASTROMOUSE!"

cried Pip.

"Can I live on the moon now?"

"But how will you get to the moon Pip?" asked Mum.
"You haven't got a rocket."

"Oh yes I have!" he squeaked excitedly. **"Look!"**

Pip had made himself a wonderful rocket out of an old funnel, sticky tape and cardboard.

But it didn't seem to want to blast off.

"Perhaps I need a launch pad," Pip thought.

The next day Pip made a launch pad out of a log and an old piece of wood. He left it at the bottom of Windy Hill.

Then he dragged his rocket all the way up to the top using an old roller skate.

Pip climbed into the rocket clutching
a bag full of biscuit crumbs (to eat
with the stinky moon cheese).

He was ready for take off!

3, 2, 1...

BLAST OFF!

Pip's rocket rolled
down the hill...

...faster and *faster*,
onto the launch pad...

...up into the
sky and then...

...down again
with a big

BUMP!

Pip's rocket was broken, his space helmet was dented and his biscuit crumbs were all over the floor.

He made his way sadly back home.

Then he saw something shining brightly in a pond.
It was the moon!

"Wow!" he cried, "I couldn't get to the moon, so the moon has come to me!"

He crept to the edge of the pond and reached down to break off a piece of stinky cheese.

But the moon didn't smell like stinky cheese.
It smelled like a stinky pond!

Suddenly two big yellow eyes
popped out of the middle of the moon.

"EEEEEEEEK!"

squeaked Pip. He ran as fast as he could, all the way home.

Mum met him at the door.

"Wherever have you been Pip?"
she cried.

"To the moon," said Pip.

"And I don't want to live there any more.
It's not made of cheese, it smells like a
stinky pond and there isn't a mouse
on the moon, there's **a frog!**"

"Well, in that case," said Mum, "would you like to live here with me instead?"

Pip gave his mum a great big hug, which of course meant...

...yes!

NEXT STEPS

Discussion and Comprehension

Discuss the story with the children and ask the following questions, encouraging them to take turns and give full answers if they are able to. Offer support by turning to the appropriate pages of the book if needed.

• What did you like most about this story?
• Why does Pip think that the moon is made of cheese?
• What is Pip's favourite meal?
• What did Pip use to make his rocket?
• Did Pip really see the moon in the pond?
• What do you think you would see if you were able to land on the moon?

What if?

Ask the children to think about and discuss what might've happened if Pip had actually made it to the moon. Ask them to write about a scenario that didn't happen in the book, but could've happened if Pip had got to the moon. Talk about ideas first and give examples – perhaps Pip met a giant mouse! Perhaps the moon really was made of stinky cheese and he ate it all! Maybe he was sad because he couldn't get home...

Give the children a large circle of yellow paper and colouring pens for them to write about and illustrate their scenarios. Encourage them to write in full sentences. This task can be extended by asking those who are able to create more than one scenario. Take some examples and read the story again changing it so that Pip does get to the moon.

Painting the moon with textured paint

Give each child a piece of black sugar paper with a large circle outlined in the middle. Make some moon paint by mixing two parts yellow paint to one part flour. Ask the children to paint inside the circle to create their moon; they can make craters with water bottle tops. To finish they can stick adhesive gold stars around the outside of the moon.

MOUSE'S FIRST NIGHT AT
MOONLIGHT SCHOOL

With a FREE
Stories Aloud
smartphone
audio book!

See inside
front cover

SIMON PUTTOCK * ALI PYE

nosy crow